JEAN ROGERS

DINOSAURS ARE 568

PICTURES BY MARYLIN HAFNER

Greenwillow Books

NEW YORK

Library of Congress Cataloging-in-Publication Data
Rogers, Jean.
Dinosaurs are 568 / by Jean Rogers;
pictures by Marylin Hafner.
p.   cm.
Summary: Raymond does not want to start going
to school, but once there he experiences the
excitement of giving book reports, learning about
dinosaurs and whales, taking part in a play,
and writing a publisher about a mistake he finds
in a reference book.
ISBN 0-688-07931-8
[1. Schools—Fiction.]
I. Hafner, Marylin, ill.   II. Title.
III. Title: Dinosaurs are five hundred sixty eight.
PZ7.R6355Di 1988
[Fic]—dc19   88-5501   CIP   AC

In memoriam to Gavin,
the biggest Roman of them all

Raymond and his mother walked over to the school to register him for kindergarten. Raymond had been sitting in a tree in his backyard, pretending he was Robinson Crusoe looking for life on his desert island. He was not one bit happy about climbing down to return to being Raymond. It was even worse when his mother made him wash his hands and face and comb his hair. He really couldn't see the use of it when he was

going to be Robinson Crusoe again the minute he got home.

"Can't I just stay here and play?" he asked.

"Oh, Raymond, you'll want to see the room
you're going to be in and meet the teacher."

Raymond knew that the sooner this chore
was done, the sooner he could get back to his
tree, so he allowed himself to be straightened
up, brushed off, and urged along to Pemberton Elementary School.

His father and he had been reading
Robinson Crusoe for the last few weeks. Raymond decided it was his very favorite story,
probably the very best one his father had ever
read to him. He kept thinking about Robinson as he scuffed along next to his mother.

They went into the school through the big
front door. A lady sitting at a desk just inside
directed them to the kindergarten room. The
school was humming with mothers and kids
of all ages. There were quite a few other boys

and girls in the kindergarten room, too. The mothers were busy filling out forms.

"I'm Mrs. Plummer," the teacher said to Raymond's mother when they came in.

"This is Raymond Arthur Wayliss." His mother pushed him forward a bit. Mrs. Plummer smiled at him.

"Welcome, Raymond. This is going to be a fine year. I'm glad you are going to be in my room. Why don't you look around while your mother fills out your card?" Raymond did as he was told. He looked into a square glass box and saw that there were two small turtles sitting on a rock. There was a yellow plastic bowl of water for their pond and some green plants growing all around it. Raymond watched the turtles for a while. They didn't move. He guessed they were asleep. There was a play sink and refrigerator, a doll, and a teddy bear sleeping in a doll bed. A big box held a lot of blocks of all shapes and sizes. There were

9

two painting easels and many jars of bright paint. It was just like play school.

Raymond sat down and thought about Robinson Crusoe until his mother said they could go.

"Goodbye, Raymond," said Mrs. Plummer as they left. "See you Monday."

As they went out of the building, Eloise Maryjane Jenkins was coming up the walk with her mother. Eloise lived around the corner from Raymond and often came to play with him. Their mothers stopped to talk.

"Are you all done?" asked Eloise. "We're just going." Raymond nodded. "I can barely wait," Eloise said. She was skipping around, pointing her toes in her Sunday shoes and pulling at her dress. "Isn't my dress pretty?" she asked finally. Raymond looked at it.

"Fine," he said.

"My Grandmama sent it for me to go to school in so I'm going to school in it."

"Fine," said Raymond again. He pulled at his mother. "Can I go home now?"

"Oh, we've got to get registered, too," said Mrs. Jenkins. "Eloise would just die if she didn't get to go to school this year." Eloise twirled around, showing off her dress again.

"Fine," muttered Raymond, but no one heard him.

"Doesn't Mrs. Plummer look like a nice teacher, Raymond? I think you are going to be a lucky kindergarten class this year!"

"Not me," said Raymond.

"Why, Raymond! What do you mean?"

"I'm not going," said Raymond.

"Of course you're going." Mrs. Wayliss said in a louder voice. "This year you're old enough to start school."

"I'm not going." Raymond spoke louder this time, too.

Mrs. Wayliss stopped right there on the sidewalk and looked at Raymond anxiously.

"What are you saying, Raymond? Didn't you like the school? Didn't you think it looked like fun to be in that room?"

"It was okay," agreed Raymond. "The teacher was okay."

Mrs. Wayliss sighed. She and Raymond continued their walk home, and soon Raymond was climbing up the tree once more to get on with being Robinson Crusoe.

2

At the dinner table, Mrs. Wayliss was telling Mr. Wayliss about school.

"Raymond is going to enjoy it so much," she said after describing the pleasant room and the pleasant teacher and all the pleasant things to play with and learn about.

Raymond looked up from his applesauce. "I'm not going to school," he said.

Mr. Wayliss laughed. "It's pretty customary, son."

"What's that?" Raymond pushed his empty bowl over to his mother. "Can I have some more, please?"

"It means that when you get to be five years old you start school by going to kindergarten, and then on to first grade, second grade, and so on up until you graduate from high school."

"Oh," said Raymond. "Well, I'm not going to school."

Mrs. Wayliss stopped spooning applesauce into Raymond's bowl. "Oh, Raymond," she cried, "why do you keep on saying that?" Before he had a chance to answer she rushed on. "You'll have *so* much fun there! You *have* to go to school. It's the law! Everyone *has* to go to school!"

Raymond's father held up his hand and gave his wife a look that Raymond knew meant let me handle this. Raymond took his bowl and began eating again.

"Listen, Raymond, are there any special reasons you don't want to go to school?" Raymond shook his head. He finished his applesauce and started to slip away from the table. "Hold on a minute here," said Mr. Wayliss. "Let's talk about this a bit. If there aren't any reasons why you don't want to go to school right now, can you tell us what you do plan to do?"

"Nothing," said Raymond. As he left he heard his father say, "Well, let's not make a big issue out of it. By tomorrow he'll be saying something else. Maybe he just isn't mature enough yet." Raymond lingered just outside the door to hear what his mother would answer.

"Oh Will, you know how well he scored on the preschool test. He was so high in everything! And he's so big, too. Why, he's already taller than practically everyone else his age. If he waits another year he's going to look like a

15

giant compared to the other children. I wonder what on earth has gotten into him to take against school like this?"

Raymond knew the answer, but it was nothing he could explain. He didn't understand what all the fuss and bother was about. It was really quite simple. He just wasn't going to school.

3

For the next few days there was no more mention made of school. But on the day Raymond was supposed to go to kindergarten for the first time, there was quite a lot of fuss and bother. Raymond had forgotten all about it when Eloise appeared at the Wayliss' door, bright and early. She was wearing her new Grandmama dress, and she had ribbons tied over each ear, making her hair stick out in fancy arcs. Raymond quite liked them.

"Aren't you ready yet?" asked Eloise.

"Oh Eloise, come on in," said Mrs. Wayliss. "Raymond is nearly ready."

Raymond looked at his mother. "She doesn't have to wait. I'm not going."

"Now Raymond, let's not have any more of this nonsense. Of course you're going. School starts this morning. Eloise has come to walk with you. Wasn't that nice of her?"

"No," said Raymond.

"Raymond Arthur Wayliss," Mrs. Wayliss said loudly, "you just stop acting this way and get yourself on to school with Eloise this minute!"

Raymond looked at his mother. Eloise was watching them both with great interest. "I'm not going to school," Raymond said. "But I don't mind walking with Eloise."

So they set off, Eloise prancing and dancing, talking a mile a minute. Raymond walked right up to the front door of the

18

school. "Goodbye," he said to the astonished Eloise. He walked home, went around to the back door, and walked into the kitchen. His mother was loading the dishwasher. She jumped when she saw him.

"Raymond," she exclaimed, "what are you doing here? Why didn't you go to school with Eloise?"

"I did. Then I came home."

"Well, you can just go right back, young man." Mrs. Wayliss had the same determined look on her face that Raymond had on his. She dried her hands, grabbed Raymond by his arm, and marched him out the front door. She didn't even take time to get a sweater. Once at the school, she ushered him into Mrs. Plummer's room. It was still early enough, and children were coming to school from all directions.

"Mrs. Plummer, here's Raymond," Mrs. Wayliss said. She was quite out of breath from hurrying. "For some reason he's resisting coming to school, but I'm sure he really doesn't mean it. Why, he's been so interested in books and things for a long time, I—"

Mrs. Plummer was wearing a bright red dress with pretty beads. She patted Mrs. Wayliss on the arm. "Just leave him, Mrs. Wayliss. This often happens. He'll settle down and be fine as soon as you leave. He's going to love school, I know. Raymond, you can just find a seat anywhere you like. Goodbye, Mrs. Wayliss. Don't worry now."

4 Raymond went over to look at the turtles.
They were still asleep. Eloise was busy with
another girl in the pretend kitchen.

Two boys were busy pulling blocks out of a
big box. Mrs. Plummer was busy showing
another boy where to hang his jacket. Raymond went back to the door and walked out.
No one saw him go. Raymond walked home
slowly, so as to make sure his mother got
there before he did. This time she really did

jump when she saw him. She scolded him, too. Quite loudly. When she calmed down she said, "Raymond, you do have to go back to school, you know. Do you want me to take you back or do you want to go by yourself?"

"I'm not going back to school," Raymond said. "I'm going out to the backyard and work on my Robinson Crusoe hut."

Mrs. Wayliss looked as if she didn't know whether to laugh or cry. "I'm going to call your father."

Raymond went out to the backyard where he worked happily for the rest of the morning. Mrs. Wayliss had a long talk with her husband on the telephone.

After lunch, Eloise and Benjamin Loftus came over to play with Raymond. At first they talked about nothing but school, but after a while they were so busy helping Raymond with the hut that they forgot about school. Raymond's mother and father must have forgotten, too, because they didn't say another word on the subject to Raymond.

Next day, though, there was more fuss and bother, and it went on all that week. Raymond's father took him to school. On the way he talked and talked to Raymond, but he didn't say anything new so Raymond didn't really listen. He was counting the number of ants he could see scurrying along the sidewalk. Ants in the grass didn't count; they had to be actually on the sidewalk. He had gotten to seventeen before he was deposited with Mrs. Plummer. She was as friendly as before and said she hoped Raymond would stay and enjoy all the things they were going to do that morning. "We're all learning to print our names," she said, smiling at Raymond. "And we're going to the gym where Mr. Drake will teach us to do some good exercises."

Mr. Wayliss left, and Raymond went over to see the turtles. They hadn't moved. Maybe they were glued to that rock. There was a list of names written on the blackboard. Raymond looked until he found his. Then he went home. On the way he met Eloise. "Raymond," she said, "you're going the wrong way. I came to get you but you'd already gone." Raymond nodded and kept on walking. "Hey, Raymond," Eloise shouted after him. "You're going to get into trouble. Lots of trouble!"

5

It turned out that Raymond was good at standing up to the trouble he got into. His mother and father tried all kinds of arguments to make him want to go to kindergarten, but they finally gave up. They decided he wasn't mature enough, despite what the tests showed, and he could stay home another year. Raymond could print all the letters of the alphabet, he could count to one hundred easily, and he could write his name.

If his mother told him how to spell the words he could write thank-yous to his grandma for the presents she sent him.

His father finished reading to him about Robinson Crusoe, and they started another good book about a whole family shipwrecked on a desert island.

In the spring Mrs. Wayliss took Raymond back to the school for some more tests.

"Raymond did so well on the tests he's going to be placed in first grade after all," Mrs. Wayliss told his father at dinner. She smiled at her son and he smiled back. Raymond was pleased that his mother was pleased. Meanwhile there was the whole summer to enjoy.

But the day came again when Mrs. Wayliss announced that it was time to go to the school and register Raymond for first grade. Raymond was cutting the crust off his toast, taking great care to get it all in one unbroken strip. After he had eaten the soft center of the bread, he carefully poked the crust into his mouth, curling it around precisely to get the whole crust in without breaking it. It took a while before he could talk. Then he said, "I'm not going." Mrs. Wayliss was busy taking the breakfast dishes off the table by then so she didn't hear him.

But when she was straightening his jacket and pushing in his shirttail, Raymond said again, "I'm not going to school." Mrs. Wayliss was kneeling down by Raymond so her face was close to his. When Raymond said that, her face turned very red. She opened her mouth to say something, but then clamped it shut so tightly Raymond heard her teeth click. She stood up and took Raymond's hand. "Come on," she said.

This time the teacher's name was Miss Reed, and she was wearing a bright blue dress with flowers on it. While his mother filled out

27

papers and Miss Reed greeted other mothers and children who were coming in, Raymond looked around. Instead of tables there were desks, and each desk had its own chair. At the back of the room there was a huge picture of a great, green beast. It was standing in a meadow, surrounded by big green plants of all sizes and shapes. The beast seemed to be looking straight at Raymond with a tiny, piercing eye. There was some printing at the bottom of the picture. Raymond could recognize the letters, but he couldn't tell what they said. He stood and looked at the beast, examining every detail very carefully.

"Are you interested in dinosaurs?" asked Miss Reed, coming up to stand beside Raymond.

"Is that a dinosaur? Is that what it says?" he asked.

"It says 'Diplodocus, a very large, extinct, herbivorous dinosaur of the Jurassic period.'"

"What's extinct?" asked Raymond.

"That means there aren't any dinosaurs alive any more. But there were many dinosaurs long ago, Raymond. We're going to read a lot about them this year. The library has some good books about dinosaurs, and we'll be reading some funny stories about them, too. Tyrannosaurus Rex and triceratops and stegosaurus."

"What's this one called?"

"Diplodocus."

"Di-plod-o-cus," Raymond repeated.

That night at dinner Mrs. Wayliss told Mr. Wayliss about going to school to register. She looked at Raymond, who was making a delicious pool of melted butter in the middle of his baked potato.

"Raymond says he's not going again," she said softly to his father.

Mr. Wayliss put down his fork, which was halfway to his mouth, and started to speak.

Before he could get out a word, Raymond looked up.

"Oh, I've changed my mind," he said. He looked at his father, who still had his mouth open, and at his mother, who was between bites. He pushed his fork into his baked potato and started smashing potato into his lake of butter.

"They have a diplodocus there," he said.

Benjamin were in Raymond's backyard when Eloise arrived. Eloise was always full of bounce, but this morning she was extra full of what her mother called Eloise's vim and vinegar.

"Hey, you guys," she shouted as she came around the side of the house. "Guess what?" She was holding the hand of another girl. "This is Kim Marie Ellsworth. She's moving into the house across the street from you, Raymond. She's just my age. She's going to be in our class. She's coming to school Monday. Her mother said I could take her around the neighborhood to meet everyone." Eloise stopped to catch her breath.

"Wanta make swords with us?" asked Raymond. "We're going to play Roman soldiers." Benjamin had brought over a bundle of laths, and he and Raymond were attaching handles to them with Mr. Wayliss' staple gun.

Mrs. Wayliss had provided the boys with cardboard boxes from her weekly grocery shopping, and Benjamin was going to draw shields on the sides. Benjamin was very good at drawing. He had brought over his book on Roman soldiers so he could make the shields the right shape.

"Girls don't play Roman soldiers," said Eloise loftily. She started to pull Kim away, but Kim said, "Yes they do, Eloise. I want a sword, don't you?" And so the girls stayed. Kim pored over the pictures in Benjamin's book while Eloise helped flatten the cardboard boxes. "If we can get some big brown paper sacks, we can make some Roman armor too," she said. It was easy to get big grocery sacks from Mrs. Wayliss. She said she would be glad to get rid of a few.

Kim took the scissors, and in a few minutes she showed Eloise and Raymond and

Benjamin how to cut a neckhole and two armholes in the paper bag. Raymond ran to his room and got his box of Magic Markers and his big roll of masking tape. With Benjamin's book to guide them, everyone was soon engrossed in decorating the pretend armor and shields. Benjamin helped the others with his good drawing.

It was Kim who thought of using the tassels of weeds for the plumes. There were plenty of these along the back fence. Raymond stuck them onto the paper hats with masking tape. The crisscrossed tape, when outlined with black dots, looked just right for Roman soldiers.

Mrs. Wayliss came out and admired their handiwork. "Benjamin is staying for lunch with Raymond. Why don't you girls run home and ask if you can stay, too?"

The four of them spent the rest of the afternoon finishing their Roman soldier outfits. Smaller paper bags made fine helmets. The swords were long and slim and just right. They made wonderful whacking sounds when they were struck together.

At the end of the afternoon, the paper costumes had been mended many times with Raymond's tape as the tide of the battle ebbed and flowed. The cardboard shields were scarred and torn, and Eloise cried only a tiny bit when her finger got whacked by a sword by mistake. Kim said she was ever so glad she had moved into the neighborhood.

When it was time to go home, she went into the house with Raymond and told Mrs. Wayliss she had had a very good time. "Thank you for the lunch," she said. "It was so nice to meet you, Mrs. Wayliss." She said goodbye then and she and Eloise went home.

Mrs. Wayliss said, "What a nice new friend

you have, Raymond. She has such pleasant manners. Put the cardboard scraps in the incinerator, dear, and then come set the table for dinner."

Monday morning Eloise called for Raymond as usual. "Hurry," she ordered, hopping around even faster than usual. "We've got to pick up Kim."

At Kim's house there were boxes all over the front room, some not even opened yet, but Kim was all ready for school. Miss Reed introduced Kim to the class, and everyone had to stand up and say their names. "Would you like to tell us where you went to school before moving here, Kim?" Miss Reed asked when the name-telling was finished.

"She lives right across the street from Raymond and she's already my friend," Eloise piped up.

"Eloise," said Miss Reed. "Why don't we let Kim tell about herself?"

"We moved here from Oregon City, Oregon," Kim said. "Before Oregon I lived in Seoul, Korea. When I was three years old I came to America to be the adopted daughter of my mother and father. When I was five years old, last year, I went to court and became a citizen of the United States of America." Kim stood up in front of the class and smiled at everyone. It was just like Raymond giving one of his reports on dinosaurs.

Eloise interrupted. "She can say things in Korean too."

"Only my name and hello, how are you, and a few things like that," Kim said. She said some very funny-sounding words. "I am getting a little brother from Korea, too," Kim went on. "Pretty soon now he will be coming on a big airplane to Oregon. Then Mother

38

will go down and get him and bring him home to be our adopted boy. He is not a year old yet. I can bring a picture of him to show you."

On the playground at recess everyone wanted to play with Kim. Raymond and Benjamin had a hard time getting enough people to play even a quick game of kickball before it was time to go back inside. When the bell rang, most of Miss Reed's class was still standing around Kim asking her questions.

7

The next day Kim brought the picture she had promised. "In this snapshot," she said, standing up in front of the class again, "he is only a few months old. We are hoping he will get here from Korea before his first birthday so he can have a birthday party with his new family. His name will be Scott Edwin Ellsworth."

"Why does it take so long for him to get here? Why don't you know when he is coming?" These were just some of the questions

Kim was asked before Miss Reed said that, interesting as all this was, it was time to get down to work.

Kim and Raymond were finished with their first lessons early, so Miss Reed told Raymond he could take Kim to the library with him and show her around. The whole class usually went to the library on Thursday afternoons to return their books and listen to a story.

"Here is the new girl in our class," Raymond told Mrs. Davis.

"Oh, yes. Welcome to our library, Kim. Do you have a special interest like Raymond does? He's our dinosaur authority."

"I like dinosaurs, too," Kim said.

Mrs. Davis smiled at Kim and Raymond. "You two will have a lot to talk about then. Raymond, will you show Kim where the 568's are?"

Raymond somehow did not feel like talking to Kim about his very favorite subject, but he took her over to the nonfiction shelves that held the library's collection of dinosaur books. He turned his back to her and looked for a book for himself.

When they were checking out their choices, Mrs. Davis handed them each a book. "Here's an exciting story for each of you," she said. "I'm sure you'll be able to read these yourselves." Raymond looked at his book. *Danger in Dinosaur Valley* was the title. He looked at Kim's book, *Escape from Tyrannosaurus*. He wished Mrs. Davis had given him that one.

He and Kim walked back to their classroom. "We can trade books when we're finished," said Kim.

"Okay," Raymond agreed. He thought he would hurry to read his story so he could trade with Kim.

The next Monday Kim gave a report, and this time it was about a dinosaur. Miss Reed said that she did well and that it was nice of her to share her information with the class.

That was exactly what she said when Raymond gave his reports. No one told Kim that Raymond had already made a report about that same dinosaur, not even Eloise. Eloise often said, "You already told us that, Raymond." Eloise was very good at remembering.

It seemed to Raymond that he could never go to the library by himself anymore. However quickly he did his work, Kim was always finished and ready to go to the library, too. One day when he and Kim were about to leave the classroom together, Miss Reed called him back. "You didn't listen to the directions carefully, Raymond. I think you had better do this lesson over." So Raymond had to stay behind, and he didn't get to go to the library at all that day.

At recess Raymond would not play kickball. "I'm not going to play with any old girls," he said. He dragged Benjamin away and wouldn't let him play with them, either.

The Friday after Thanksgiving Raymond was at Benjamin's house. He was going to sleep over. Benjamin's mother said they could put up the two-man tent on the sun porch and pretend they were out camping. They were going to eat their dinners out in the tent, too. Eloise and Kim came by. They were bursting with excitement.

"Guess what, Raymond," Eloise shouted as they came up the stairs. "Guess what, Benjamin!"

"We got a telephone call," Kim said. Her eyes were shining and she was smiling with a very big smile. "Tomorrow my mother is going to get my baby brother. He's here! He came on the plane from Korea just like I did. Mother's coming back with him on Sunday."

"We can't stay and play," said Eloise. "Kim's mother is letting us unpack all the baby clothes she has. Her dad is setting up the crib in Kim's room right now, so we've got to hurry back and help."

"Scott is going to sleep in my room at first so he won't feel lonely," Kim said. "Then Daddy is going to fix our attic to have two bedrooms, one for each of us."

On Monday the whole class got to share Kim's happy news. She brought a new picture of her baby brother and passed it around. "I wanted to bring him to school so you could all meet him," Kim said, "but Mother said he needed some time to get used to us and all the new things in his life first. Then she will bring him for a visit. He's a very good baby," Kim went on proudly. "He didn't cry at all last night. And this morning at breakfast he smiled. My mother told me that when I first came from Korea, I hid my face when anyone looked at me because I felt so shy. I don't remember that at all. The only thing I can remember is the big airplane. That was very scary."

45

Every morning for quite a while, Kim had something to share with the class about the new baby in her family. If she forgot a single thing, Eloise reminded her. Raymond and Benjamin were invited to meet the baby, but Mrs. Wayliss told them not to stay very long. Raymond thought this was silly advice. Who would want to waste time on a little old baby? Benjamin had two smaller sisters, so he was used to babies. One quick look and he was ready to leave with Raymond. About all you could see anyway was a little dark head.

But something rather strange happened to Raymond a few days later. He and Benjamin were at Kim's, and Scott was awake.

"Would you like to hold him?" Mrs. Ellsworth asked Raymond. Raymond didn't know what to say. The next thing he knew, a warm and wiggly Scott was thrust into his somewhat unwilling arms.

"Hold on tight," Mrs. Ellsworth said, beaming. "He's really a big, strong boy." In spite of himself Raymond thought the baby had a nice, soft smell. Kim and Eloise knelt down by Raymond and made goo-goo noises at Scott. He laughed and waved his arms.

"Here," said Raymond shortly. "Benjamin and I have things to do." When the boys left, the girls were down on the floor showing Scott how to crawl. There was a lot of giggling going on. At the door Mrs. Ellsworth thanked them for stopping by.

"It's so nice that Kim and her friends make it so interesting for Scott," she said gratefully.

"Yuck," muttered Raymond as she shut the door. But that night as he was going to sleep, Raymond thought about Kim's baby brother. It might not be so bad to have a baby brother. He sighed as he turned over. If only Kim didn't talk so much about him.

8

March 9th was Raymond's birthday. It seemed to him that every single person in his room had already turned seven. He had waited so long for March to come that when it did he'd forgotten all about his birthday. He was quite surprised when his mother said, "Let's make out your birthday list this morning, Raymond. You may make a choice this year. You may invite a lot of friends for ice cream and cake, or you may have a few friends in and Dad and I will take you all out for a hamburger and the movies."

"That's what I'd like," said Raymond promptly. "How many is a few?"

Mrs. Wayliss laughed. "Well, I thought you could ask Kim and Eloise and Benjamin, of course. And Benjamin can sleep over if you two don't get too silly and excited."

Raymond nodded slowly. "Benjamin and Eloise are enough," he said. "You don't have to ask Kim."

"Raymond," Mrs. Wayliss said, "of course you must ask Kim. She's one of your best friends."

"No, she's not," said Raymond. "I don't want to invite her."

"But Raymond, she asked you to her party! And just last month Kim invited you to share her brother's first birthday cake. Why don't you want to ask Kim?"

"She's always talking," Raymond said.

"Oh, for heaven's sake, how can you say that! Why, Kim is the nicest, politest friend you have."

Raymond couldn't very well say that was part of the trouble, so he didn't say anything.

"She doesn't talk nearly as much as Eloise. You're going to invite Kim and that's final!"

Raymond looked at his mother to see if it would be worthwhile to make more fuss. Clearly, it wouldn't do any good. He didn't want his mother to say he couldn't have a party at all. "Well, okay," Raymond said.

"Good," replied his mother. "Why don't you sit down right now and fill out these invitations with some of that improved writing Miss Reed has been telling me about."

As soon as Raymond filled in all the spaces on the invitations telling where to come and when to come, he wrote his friends' names on the envelopes. "Now you run and deliver your invitations," his mother said. "I'll make

cupcakes for your whole class on Wednes-
day."

Raymond walked past Kim's house and
went first to Benjamin's. His mother said
there was no reason Benjamin couldn't sleep
over the night of the party. Benjamin said he
would come with Raymond to deliver the
other invitations to the girls.

"Not until you've picked up your room," his
mother said.

"Wait for me," Benjamin said to Raymond.
"It'll only take me a minute."

"No shoving it under the bed, Benjamin,
and I mean it. I find anything under the bed
and it's all over."

"I'll help you," offered Raymond.

"Well, don't go up there and start playing,
you two. I'm going to check it out before Benjamin steps one inch away from this house."
Benjamin's mother didn't smile one bit.

Raymond thought Benjamin's room didn't

look half bad. He offered to put the Leggo blocks back in their bin while Benjamin dug stuff out from under his bed. "I had a real neat spaceship but Marcie came in and knocked it over," Benjamin said. "She ought to pick it up, but Mom says she's too little to know better."

"I don't mind," Raymond said. Benjamin carried his dirty clothes out to the laundry chute. He took his drawing pad and markers off his bed and smoothed the cover. He opened his bottom dresser drawer and stuffed in a few toys. He stacked all the books into a neat pile on his desk and started another pile for magazines and papers. Raymond found a rather squashed fig cookie, the soft kind, under the last pile of blocks. He brushed it off carefully, decided it wasn't too dried out, and offered to share it with Benjamin. It had a definitely dusty taste, but that disappeared with strong chewing.

"Okay, Mom," Benjamin called down the stairs. "I'm done, come and check."

Mrs. Loftus came up the stairs, putting her feet down hard to make a lot of noise. "Here comes the giant, clomp, clomp," she called. "And this giant eats boys with messy rooms for lunch. So there better not be a boy up here with a messy room!" She stuck her head around Benjamin's door. "Hey, it looks like someone could just possibly live in this room! Did you by any chance push everything into the closet?"

Benjamin opened the closet door. "Nothing. Nothing on the floor and nothing under the bed."

"The vacuum and dusting person says okay, you can go. Stick your invitation on the bulletin board as you go out, Benjy, so I won't forget."

Eloise was already at Kim's house, so Raymond left the invitation with her mother.

Walking back to Kim's, he thought about leaving the invitation in his pocket. He could tell his mother he had forgotten it or lost it, but he knew his mother had extra invitations and he would just have to write it all out again. Besides, as soon as Eloise saw her invitation, she would be right over to talk to Kim, and if Kim hadn't gotten one Eloise would probably go straight to Raymond's house to find out why.

In front of Kim's house Raymond said to Benjamin, "Let's go over to my house first. I'll do this later." He stuffed Kim's invitation into his pocket.

Benjamin stayed for lunch and spent the afternoon with Raymond. It wasn't until Raymond was setting the table for dinner that his mother said, "Get all your invitations delivered this morning, hon?" For a moment Raymond pretended he didn't hear her.

"Well—almost," he said slowly. Mrs. Wayliss looked at Raymond sharply. "Raymond," she said sternly, "you go right across the street this minute and invite Kim to your party! What's gotten into you today?" So that was that.

The party was fine. Mrs. Wayliss took them to the movies in the afternoon. Afterward, Mr. Wayliss joined them and they all had hamburgers and French fries. "Have all you want to eat," said Raymond's father, "but don't forget to save room for the cake and ice cream when we get home."

After the birthday candles had been blown out, Raymond opened his presents. Eloise had brought him a bright yellow flashlight with a set of batteries. "I knew you'd like it," she beamed.

Benjamin's present was a hammer, a real one. Mr. Wayliss said he was really pleased to see that. "Now maybe my hammer will stay on my workbench."

"Oh no, Mr. Wayliss," Benjamin said, "Raymond and I often need two hammers."

"Well," Mr. Wayliss laughed, "I'll have to see that you get a hammer for *your* birthday, Benjamin."

Kim's present was in a long box. "This is something you are going to like, too," Eloise said. "Hurry up and open it." Inside the box there were a lot of smooth pieces of wood cut into different shapes and sizes like a puzzle. You could tell by looking at the picture on the box that if you put all the pieces together, it made the skeleton of a stegosaurus.

"It's a model of a real stegosaurus," Kim said. "My mother sent to the Smithsonian Institute for it."

"Think you can put it together without my help?" asked Raymond's father.

"Yes, I can," Raymond said firmly.

"If he gets stuck I can help him," said Benjamin.

"Raymond is good at making things," Kim broke in. "He won't have any trouble."

Raymond looked again at the picture on the box lid and all the tiny pieces in the box. Each piece fit along the backbone of the stegosaurus, so you could take it all apart and put it together again. Maybe he and Benjamin could start on it tonight before they went to bed.

There was a long silence. "Raymond," Mrs. Wayliss said with that tone of voice that Raymond knew very well meant "haven't you forgotten something?" He opened his mouth to say thank you to Kim as nicely as he had to Eloise and Benjamin. Something seemed to have gotten stuck in his throat. Finally he managed to croak out a thank you. Mrs. Wayliss gave him a look. "Raymond is going to love this," she said to Kim. "Now, how about some more cake and ice cream?"

9

"Class," said Miss Reed. "Pemberton Elementary School's Spring Festival is really upon us. We'll be giving a play. We're all going to work hard and get our regular lessons done as fast as we can so we'll have time to work on our play. Some of the fifth graders from Mrs. Fallon's room are going to help us with our stage scenery and our costumes. We'll help them during our art period.

Now let's read the play and then I'll assign the parts."

Everyone was very excited about the play and wanted to know right away who was going to get the parts. "Settle down now," warned Miss Reed. "Everyone is going to have something to do, don't worry. The play we are doing is called *Taro the Fisherman*. It is based on a Japanese folk tale. Now, let's read the play." Miss Reed passed out all the copies of the play she had, and everyone had a chance to read a bit of it aloud. All the boys wanted to be Taro, but Miss Reed said Philip Shimizu would be the very best Taro because he was Japanese.

Raymond thought he would like to be the old Sea King or Big Turtle, but Miss Reed gave out all the parts and Raymond didn't get one. Benjamin was head of the costume crew, Eloise was A Girl, and Kim was Princess Sea Star. When Miss Reed listed all the people who were going to be Sea Citizens, Raymond wasn't among them, either. All the jobs were given out—helping with costumes, collecting props, prompter, everything. No one noticed that Raymond hadn't been given a thing to do. Not even Eloise. Finally, just as it was time for recess, Raymond called out, "Miss Reed. You left me out!"

"Why, Raymond!" Miss Reed clapped her hand to her head just as the bell rang. "Just a minute, class. I've given you a very important and responsible job, Raymond. You're going to be our announcer. You always speak up loud and clear so we're depending on you to do a good job."

The entire class enjoyed getting ready for the Spring Festival and the play. There was plenty to do, so everyone could help. The costume committee decided to make all the costumes from the big rolls of colored paper in the supply room. Benjamin and some of the students from Mrs. Fallon's room drew pictures of all the costumes. Ernest, on the props committee, gathered up all the things needed in the play. Kim and Raymond helped the scenery crew of fifth graders make paper rocks for the first scene and seaweed for the underwater part of the play.

Eloise and Benjamin drew paper flowers to decorate the stage, and while the people who had speaking parts practiced their lines in the front of the room, those who didn't helped cut out the flowers. After the first two practices, Miss Reed said Raymond didn't need to go through his whole introduction every time there was a rehearsal. "We can see you will do your part splendidly when the time comes, Raymond." In the meantime, he was very happy to paint rocks and walls for the undersea kingdom.

The Spring Festival assembly was Thursday morning. About halfway through it, Miss Reed's class had to tiptoe out and go behind the stage to get ready for their play. The paper costumes, the box of props, the rolls of paper that made the scenery were all ready and waiting. Judy the aide was helping Miss Reed backstage. Miss Reed kept shushing everyone behind the curtain because out in front the program was still going on.

Raymond was all dressed up in his very best clothes. He had his introduction paper in his hand. He was ready to go on the moment Miss Reed gave him the signal. When the curtain opened, he stepped out and told about the play, announced all the players, and thanked the people in Miss Fallon's class who had helped out. When he bowed, just exactly as Miss Reed had told him to, he was filled with pleasure at the thought that he would get to do it all over again that afternoon.

All went well until it was time for Taro to mount the back of Big Turtle and ride off to the Sea King's palace. Philip was very small and Justin was the biggest boy in the class, even if he wasn't as tall as Raymond. In rehearsals, his broad back carried Philip easily across the stage and into the undersea palace. Since the costumes were paper and tore easily, Miss Reed said they wouldn't use them for rehearsals. Now Philip was having a difficult time staying on Justin's back as Justin pretended to be a big old green turtle. The paper kept slipping and sliding, and Philip was trying to be so careful not to tear it that he almost forgot what he was doing. Miss Reed hissed at them just to get up and walk, but she couldn't hiss loud enough to make them hear without letting the audience out in front hear it, too.

Kim, the Mermaid Sea Princess, was also having trouble with her paper fish tail. Although her feet stuck out at the bottom under the fin, the opening was so narrow that Kim could barely move. Fortunately she didn't have to walk anyplace, but it was difficult to stand. She teetered perilously. She couldn't sit because the paper was too stiff. Raymond watched all this from the wings, waiting until it was all over and he was to walk out and make the farewell announcement and thank everyone for coming. The Sea King's crown tipped over one eye, and his long beard of paper curls rode up to cover the other eye so that when he was to shake hands with Taro and wish him farewell, he missed Taro's outstretched hand. This delighted the audience, who was even more delighted when Taro tried to ride on Big Turtle's slippery paper back, and the whole thing came off in his hands.

But back in the room Miss Reed said they had all done fine. When she suggested that in the afternoon performance Taro should just walk alongside Turtle, pretending to ride, Raymond raised his hand. "I know how to fix the costumes," he said. "We just need some masking tape."

"Oh yes," cried Eloise, "Raymond does that all the time with our Roman costumes." Then Kim and Benjamin jumped in and told how Raymond with his ever-ready roll of masking tape could make their paper costumes stick to them really well.

That afternoon in the performing arts room, the friends and parents of Miss Reed's first grade filled all the chairs and some extras borrowed from the projection room. Raymond tucked in his shirt tail without being told and gave a fine, loud introduction to the play. Taro rode Big Turtle, whose shell was firmly in place, above and below, stuck fast with cleverly hidden sticky tape. Princess Sea Star was firmly propped up against the largest rock, the tears in her costume carefully mended.

The play was a big success. Afterward there was punch and cookies and the fifth graders who had helped came down and had refreshments, too. As Raymond's mother was waiting for him to collect his jacket, Eloise told her all about Raymond's good idea. Kim helped her tell it. Then Miss Reed heard them talking and came over and said, "Yes, Mrs. Wayliss, Raymond really saved the day!" As he walked home with his mother, Raymond thought that school was certainly a wonderful place. It was lucky he had decided to go after all.

10

One day when Raymond was in the library browsing, Mrs. Davis showed him a book on the blue whale. "I'm sure you'll enjoy reading about this mammal," she said. "It's the largest animal that ever lived. Even bigger than the dinosaurs." Mrs. Davis was right. Raymond more than enjoyed it, he fell in love with the blue whale. He also liked to read about dolphins, porpoises, fish, crabs, and all the other things that live in the sea.

Mr. Wayliss said he was really glad to have a change from deserts and extinct beasts, and to learn so much with Raymond about the oceans of the world and all the interesting creatures that could be found there. Kim began reading about seashells and started a collection.

When she brought her shells to school to show them off, Raymond grudgingly agreed she gave a good report. Privately he thought seashells were not nearly as exciting as live sea animals. He just hoped Kim would stick to seashells.

During Easter vacation Raymond and his father visited the aquarium in Seattle. The biggest fish there was a shark, but there were lots of pictures of whales, and beside a tank there was a microscope to look at plankton magnified.

Raymond told the class all about it. "Plankton are masses of tiny, tiny simple animal and plant organisms that float in the ocean. When you look at them in the water, you can't even see them, but if you look at them under a microscope, you can tell they are all different shapes and sizes. Isn't it interesting that the biggest animal in the world makes a meal on these tiny little microscopic bits? Because that's what the blue whale does." Then he went on to tell the class how the large whales strain the water back out of their mouths with their baleen strainers. He showed them some of the pictures in the book. Everyone said it was the best report Raymond had ever given.

The next time he went to the library, Mrs. Davis showed Raymond a brand-new book. It was called the *Encyclopedia of Fascinating Facts about Fish and Other Creatures of the Sea*. Raymond was the very first person to check it out. There were lots and lots of photographs and drawings, some in color and some black and white. There was a paragraph about each picture, and Raymond agreed it was fascinating. He took the book home and spent his evening looking and reading. He carried it back to school with him the next day so he would be able to dip into it when he had some spare time.

When the class went to the library, Raymond was still enjoying the book. He spent the weekend reading more fascinating facts. Benjamin was away all Saturday and Sunday, and Kim and Eloise were busy with each other. They did come to see if Raymond wanted to wheel Scott in his push cart, but they didn't mind when he said he wanted to read instead.

Monday morning Raymond rushed through his breakfast so he could get to school early. He went right down to the library with the big book. "Mrs. Davis," he said, "Mrs. Davis, there's a mistake in this book."

"Why, what is it, Raymond? What do you mean?"

"It says here that all whales have a single blow hole. But Mrs. Davis, it's only the toothed whales that have one blow hole. All baleen whales have two blow holes. That's how whalers in the early days knew when they saw a great whale, by its V-shaped blow or double spout. That's really their nose holes, where they push out the air they've breathed when they come up for more air. They have flaps that close over these holes so water can't get in when they dive." Raymond was so excited he just couldn't talk fast enough. "I read it in the other encyclopedia and the sea mammal book. There's even a picture." Raymond was shocked to think that a book in the library could have a mistake in

71

it. "They should check their facts," he said, "before they go putting them in a book!"

"Run on to your class before you're late," Mrs. Davis told him. "I'll look into it. Why don't you leave the book here?" Raymond showed Mrs. Davis the picture of the big blue whale with the caption underneath that had the mistake.

Mrs. Davis looked in several other books and found that Raymond was correct. When he came down to the library after school she said, "I have an idea, Raymond. Why don't you write to the publisher of this book and tell him about the error? Companies that publish encyclopedias do like to have all their facts straight, I'm sure. If you will write a letter at home tonight, tomorrow I will show you how to put in the sources you can quote from. Then you can copy it over and we'll send it off."

Raymond knew just what he wanted to

say. "Dear Editor of the Encyclopedia of Fascinating Facts about Fish and Other Creatures of the Sea, I don't think you should tell things about whales that aren't true in your book. I think you should check all your facts and make sure they are really right because the kids who read your book think it is okay and true. All the books in the library should be true unless it is a made-up story. On page 157 of your book there is a mistake. The big blue whale is a baleen whale and it has two blow holes. All baleen whales have two blow holes. It is the toothed whales that have one blow hole. There are several kinds of baleen whales and they all have two blow holes."

When Mrs. Davis read Raymond's letter, she said she thought he had done a very good job of explaining. She told him to put in the names of the encyclopedia and sea mammal book from which he had learned that all baleen whales have a double blow hole. "Put down the page number, too," she advised him. Raymond worked hard on his letter and by the time he went home that afternoon it was ready to go to the post office. The publishing company's office was way off in Chicago, Illinois, so Mrs. Davis warned Raymond that it might take quite a long time before he could expect an answer. After three days it seemed quite long enough to Raymond to get a letter from anyplace, but no letter came so Raymond forgot all about it. Spring had come and there were plenty of other things to occupy him.

The Kenton Journal

LOCAL YOUTH FINDS MISTAKE IN NATIONAL ENCYCLOPEDIA

Raymond Wayliss First Grade Pupil at Pemberton Elementary School Catches Up the Experts

Teacher Encouraged Him to Write

OOK ART DIRECTOR iven Award

11

On April 26th, something very interesting happened. When Raymond came home from school, his mother told him he had received a letter from the Karelia Educational Press. "What did they say?" asked Raymond.

"I thought you would want to open it yourself," she replied.

On the front of the long envelope Raymond saw his name and address. Inside was a letter that said, "Dear Raymond, We surely did appreciate your letter about our *Fascinating Facts About Fish and Other Creatures of the Sea.* Here at Karelia Press we try very hard to make every fact in our books correct. Several editors go over the material very carefully, and the copy editor tries to check that everything we print is accurate. We agree with you that our readers expect our facts to be correct and that we owe it to them to be dependable in this regard.

"We are happy to find that you have been reading our encyclopedia so carefully. We like to hear from our readers even when they are critical. In that way we can continue to serve them to the best of our ability.

"Please rest assured, Raymond, that when this book is reprinted, the error you have pointed out to us will be rectified. A second edition of this encyclopedia is scheduled to be published early next year. As soon as it is, we will be happy to send you a copy of the revised edition. Thank you again for your letter. Yours sincerely, James S. Ribar, Director, Public Relations and Sales Management, Karelia Educational Press."

"What does rectified mean?" Raymond asked his mother when she finished reading him the letter.

"To make something right, to correct it. I must say, Raymond, that's a very nice letter. I'm impressed." And Raymond's mother gave him a kiss and a pat on the back. Mr. Wayliss was pleased when he came home from work and saw the letter, and Raymond went to bed that night with a very satisfied feeling.

The next day Miss Reed shared Raymond's letter with the class before he took it down to the library to show Mrs. Davis. She liked it, too. After morning recess Miss Reed said the *Kenton Journal* was going to send a reporter over to the school to talk to Raymond about the letter. She had telephoned them, and they thought it would make a good story for the paper. Just before lunchtime, Raymond was called to the principal's office. "And bring your letter," the intercom said.

The newspaper reporter asked Raymond a lot of questions. "Did you write the letter yourself? Was it your own idea? Did you find the mistake yourself?" And a lot of other questions. There was a girl with the reporter, and every time Raymond opened his mouth to answer a question, she took a picture. She asked Raymond to hold up a copy of the encyclopedia with one hand and the letter he received from the publisher with the other. It was getting pretty boring before they finally finished asking questions and taking pictures. Raymond almost missed his lunch.

That evening his picture was in the paper with a long story. Above the picture it said "Local Youth Finds Mistake in National Encyclopedia." Alongside the picture it said,

"Raymond Wayliss, first grade pupil at Pemberton Elementary School catches up the experts." Then under that there was a story all about Raymond, his interest in whales, his interest in books, how Mrs. Davis had encouraged him to write, but how he had found the mistake all by himself.

The next day everyone wanted to talk to Raymond. The principal cut the story out of the paper and put it up on the wall just outside the office so everyone could see it, and Mrs. Davis tacked a copy on the library bulletin board, as well. Miss Reed told the class how proud she was of Raymond, and they all agreed.

Raymond's parents were even more proud. Mr. Wayliss went down to the *Kenton Journal*'s office and bought a whole bunch of newspapers so they could send copies to all the relatives. Mrs. Wayliss took several pictures of Raymond holding up the page with his picture and the story.

That night at bedtime when Mr. Wayliss finished reading the book he and Raymond were sharing he said, "Well son, it's been a big day for us all, hasn't it?"

Raymond nodded sleepily. "I'm sure glad," his father said as he tucked Raymond in and turned out the light, "that you decided to go to school. I wouldn't have wanted to miss diplodocus or any of those other dinosaurs or the whales we read about. And just think what a lot we still have to enjoy, son."

When Mr. Wayliss turned out the light, Raymond was already asleep with a smile on his face.

DINOSAURS

ARE 5 6 8